Frédéric

Leo Lionni

Petite bibliothèque de l'école des loisirs
11, rue de Sèvres, Paris 6e

En bordure d'une prairie il y avait un vieux mur de pierres.

Dans ce mur, près d'une grange et d'un grenier à grains,
une famille de joyeux mulots s'était installée.

Mais les fermiers avaient abandonné la grange
et le grenier était vide.
Comme l'hiver approchait, les petits mulots entreprirent alors
d'amasser du maïs et des noisettes, de la paille et du blé.
Ils travaillaient tous, nuit et jour. Tous… sauf Frédéric.

« Frédéric, pourquoi ne travailles-tu pas ? »
« Mais si, je travaille », répondit-il.
« Je fais provision de soleil pour l'hiver,
quand il fera froid et sombre. »

Et quand ils virent Frédéric, assis là, à regarder la prairie,
ils lui dirent :
« Et maintenant, Frédéric, qu'est-ce que tu fais ? »
Il répondit simplement : « Je fais provision de couleurs pour l'hiver gris. »

Un jour que Frédéric semblait à moitié endormi,
ils lui demandèrent sur un ton de reproche s'il n'était pas en train de rêver.
«Oh non!» répondit-il, «je fais provision de mots…
parce que l'hiver sera long et nous ne saurons plus quoi nous dire.»

L'hiver arriva.
À la première neige les cinq petits mulots
se mirent à l'abri sous les pierres.

Au début, les mulots avaient
de quoi manger
et ils savaient assez d'histoires de renards
stupides et de gros méchants chats
pour se distraire…
c'était une famille heureuse.

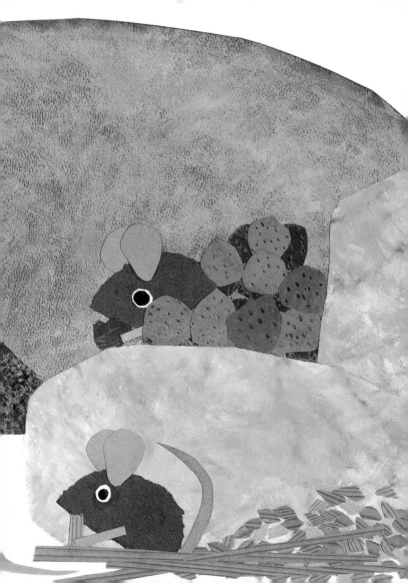

Mais petit à petit ils grignotèrent
les baies et les noisettes ;
ils épuisèrent leur provision de paille.
Le blé n'était plus pour eux
qu'un souvenir.
Il faisait froid et personne
n'avait plus envie
de faire des parlottes.

Alors les mulots se rappelèrent
ce que Frédéric leur avait dit
du soleil, des couleurs
et des mots.
« Et tes provisions,
Frédéric ? »
demandèrent-ils.

«Fermez les yeux!» dit Frédéric en grimpant
sur une grosse pierre.
«Voilà! Maintenant je vais vous envoyer
des rayons de soleil. Sentez-vous
comme ils sont chauds et doux,
et dorés?...»
Et, pendant que Frédéric
parlait, les quatre petits
mulots peu à peu se
réchauffaient.
Était-ce la voix
de Frédéric?
Était-ce
de la
magie?

« Et les couleurs, Frédéric ? »
lui demandèrent-ils, inquiets.
« Fermez encore les yeux ! »
Et quand il leur parla des pervenches
bleues, des coquelicots rouges
dans les blés jaunes et des petites
feuilles vertes des buissons,
ils virent les couleurs
aussi nettement
que si elles avaient
été peintes
dans leur tête.

«Et les mots, Frédéric?»
Frédéric s'éclaircit la voix,
marqua un temps de silence et,
comme du haut
d'une estrade, il dit:

Royal Mews. Buckingham Palace Rd., SW1; Tel. 0207/930 4832. Mon–Thur noon–4pm. Adult £4.20, child £2.10, under 5 yrs. free.

St. Paul's Cathedral. EC4; Tel. 0207/248 2705. Mon–Sat 8:30am–4pm (galleries open at 9:30am). Adult £5, child £2.50.

Science Museum. Exhibition Rd., SW7; Tel. 0207/938-8008. Daily 10am–6pm. Adult £6.50, child £3.50, under 5 yrs. free.

Shakespeare's Globe Theatre and Exhibition. 1 Bear Gardens, Bankside, SE1; Tel. 0207/928 6706. Daily 10am–5pm. Adult £5, child £3.

Sir John Soane's Museum. 13 Lincoln's Inn Fields, WC2; Tel. 0207/430 0175. Tues–Sat 10am–5pm. Free.

Tate Gallery Millbank. SW1; Tel. 0207/887 8000. Daily 10am–5:50pm. Free.

Tate Modern. 25 Sumner St., SE1; Tel. 0207/887 8000. Opens May 12, 2000. Sun–Thur 10am–6pm, Fri–Sat 10am–10pm. Free.

Theatre Museum. Russell St., WC2; Tel. 0207/836 2330. Tues–Sun 11am–7pm. Adult £4.50, child free.

Tower of London. EC3; Tel. 0207/709 0765. Mar–Oct Mon–Sat 9am–5pm, Sun 10am–5pm, Nov–Feb Sun–Mon 10am–4pm, Tues–Sat 9am–4pm. Adult £10.50, child £6.90, under 5 yrs. free.

Victoria and Albert Museum. Cromwell Rd., SW7; Tel. 0207/938 8500. Tues–Sun 10am–5:50pm, Mon noon–5:50pm. Adult £5, child free.

Wallace Collection. Hertford House, Manchester Square, W1; Tel. 0207/935 0687. Mon–Sat 10am–5pm, Sun 2–5pm. Free.

Westminster Abbey. Parliament Square, SW1; Tel. 0207/222 5152 or 7170. Mon–Fri 9:30am–3:45pm, Sat 9:30am–1:45pm. Closed to sightseers Sun. Call before visiting as sudden closures are frequent. Adult £5, child £2.

WHAT TO DO

What isn't there to do in London? It has something for everyone, but most especially those with time and money. It's nothing new: As a 13th-century writer put it, "Nothing is certain in London but expense." Yet the high prices on the high streets of London don't seem to stop anyone here, tourist and citizen alike, from shopping until dropping.

SHOPPING

If you can't find what you're looking for in London, you probably can't find it anywhere. The great trading tradition of this city continues into the 21st century, with every kind of shop and goods imaginable within reach. The costs are higher than you'll find in Europe and the States, thanks to the crushing VAT (Value Added Tax) and the lack of competitive pricing, but the variety, choice, and quality of goods are impressive nevertheless. Luckily, the stores have two big sales each year, one in July, and one in January.

Where to Shop

The oldest and most elegant shopping area is around Mayfair and St James's. Bond Street has a formidable collection of designer boutiques, jewelry stores, expensive stationary shops, and antique and fine art emporia. Regent Street has the famous Liberty Department store (214 Regent St.), Hamleys toy store (188–196 Regent St.), and others that specialize in such offerings as English woolens and raincoats, china, and linen stores. Jermyn and St James's streets have the highest concentration of elegant "bespoke" clothing and shoes, items that are so finely wrought that people are willing to wait months, sometimes years, and pay the earth for the privilege of ownership. If you only want the basics,

An international conglomerate of trendy shops, multi-cultural cuisine, and more — Soho never ceases to satisfy.

Oxford Street is home to the big department stores: John Lewis (278–306 Oxford St.), C&A (200 Oxford St.), Debenhams (334–348 Oxford St.), and Marks and Spencer (458 Oxford St.), where much of England buys its underwear. Selfridge's (400 Oxford St.) is a little more upmarket, with designer clothes, cosmetics, and other luxury goods.

Harrods (87–135 Brompton Rd.) and Harvey Nichols (109–123 Knightsbridge) are the big department stores in Knightsbridge, "Harvey Nicks" being decidedly more fashionable than sprawling old Harrods. The emphasis is on high fashion along Sloane Street and Beauchamp Place, where shop after shop specializes in big name designers. Chelsea offers the trend-setting King's Road, and Fulham Road has a fair share of designer boutiques and antique stores. Kensington High Street is a slightly more interesting version of Oxford Street, while Kensington Church Street is the place for antique-seekers.

When to Shop

Most shops open somewhere between 9 and 10am until 5:30 or 6pm Monday to Saturday, though some Mayfair shops close on Saturday afternoon. Traditionally there is late-night shopping in Knightsbridge on Wednesday until 7pm, and in Oxford Street and Regent Street on Thursday until 7:30 or 8pm. Many shops, however, are starting to stay open a bit later, especially bookstores — the new Piccadilly branch of Waterstone's Book Store (203 Piccadilly) has (for England) extremely generous opening hours of 8:30am to 11pm. Covent Garden shops have always kept late hours, most of them staying open from 10am to 8pm Monday to Saturday, and many open from noon to 5pm on Sunday, too. Many stores on the King's Road and some of the High streets are starting to keep Sunday hours as well, but don't take anything for granted — call first to check.

Street Markets

If you want to catch the real flavor of London shopping and some of its most colorful characters, then you should head for one of the city's many streetmarkets.

Portobello Road (Notting Hill) is always popular; on Saturday there are stalls filled with all types of antiques, bric-a-brac, and (at the Ladbroke Grove end) lots of clothing and miscellaneous bargains; fruit and vegetables are offered on weekdays.

Petticoat Lane (Middlesex Street, in the East End) is the place for shopping on Sunday, when you'll find a wide variety of goods, including lots of leather. Adjacent is the even more colorful, and chaotic, **Brick Lane Market,** where second-hand bargains abound among the curry houses and cockney "caffs" of the neighborhood.

Covent Garden's **Jubilee Market** is very popular with both tourists and locals. You can find antiques on Monday; crafts, clothes, and food Tuesday to Friday; and hand-made crafts on the weekend.

There are two north London markets that are well worth the trip. **Camden Passage** in Islington (Wednesday and Saturday for antiques, Thursdays for books, prints, and drawings) is set in the courtyard of a permanent established antique center. **Camden Lock Market,** just north of Regent's Park, is a youthful weekend market for arts and crafts, antiques, bric-a-brac, health foods, and jewelry.

The **New Caledonian Market** at Bermondsey Square (near London Bridge south of the river) is the place for serious antique collectors. The dealers are here before trading starts at 5 or 6am each Friday, and by breakfast time the best bargains have gone.

For a comprehensive list of street markets ask at tourist information offices for their brochure "Markets in London."

Best Buys

Antiques. It's easy to be fooled, so look for the seal of the professional associations LAPADA and BADA. If you find formal antique shopping a little intimidating or too expensive, try market centers such as: Alfie's Antique Market (Church Street, Marylebone), Gray's Market (Davies Street, next to Bond Street underground station), Bond Street Antique Centre (New Bond Street), or Antiquarius and Chelsea Antique Market (on King's Road). Don't be afraid to bargain, especially if you can pay in cash.

Books. Charing Cross Road is a mecca for second-hand and rare volumes, as well as some of the chain stores. "Europe's largest bookstore," the new multi-story Waterstone's (203 Piccadilly) is London's first book superstore, with juice bar, café, and restaurant. Hatchards (187 Piccadilly) has been selling books since 1797. There are a lot of specialty bookstores too, look in the *Yellow Pages*.

Clothing. Savile Row and St. James's fill most upper-crust masculine requirements from head (a ceremonial top hat at James Lock, 6 St. James's St.) to toe (hand-made shoes at John Lobb, 90 Jermyn St.). King's Road, Covent Garden, South Molton Street, Bond Street, and Knightsbridge are for the stylish, while those in search of good-quality, typically British garb, need go no farther than Marks & Spencer (458 Oxford St. and branches) or, particularly for woolens, the Scotch House (84-86 Regent St. and branches).

Fabrics. Oxford Street's John Lewis (278–306 Oxford St.) and its brother store Peter Jones (Sloane Square) have a good everyday range, but Liberty is world famous for their prints, and it is always a pleasure to visit their beautiful, galleried store at 214 Regent St.

Perfumes. Stay on Jermyn Street for altogether sweeter smells at Floris (89 Jermyn St.), purveyors of perfume since 1730. Crown

In search of a particular edition or specialty book? Chances are you'll find it in one of London's many book sellers.

Perfumery at 51 Burlington Arcade (on Piccadilly) has the old recipes of exquisite perfumes and colognes worn by English royalty and legends; the more modern-minded should try Jo Malone's store (150 Sloane Street) for her wide range of scents.

Rainwear. You will probably need some protection from the elements while in London, so if there's a sale on, pick up one of the famous red and beige checked raincoats by Burberry's (165 Regent St.).

ENTERTAINMENT

More goes on in London in a day than in a year in most places. Just try reading all the reviews and events in the London listings magazines for a single week. For weekly details of all London's entertainment look in the listings magazines published each Wednesday (*Time Out* or *What's On*), or the *Evening Standard's* Thursday magazine supplement *Hot Tickets*.

For many visitors to London the **theater** is what makes the city special. There are some 43 functioning mainstream theaters in central London alone. Most of these are in the West End, staging comedies, musicals, and dramas of varying degrees of greatness. Other theaters include the National Theatre at the South Bank Centre, which stages innovative productions of the classics, some excellent modern pieces, and the occasional rousing musical revival. The Old Vic (next to Waterloo station), specializes in revivals of the classics, although it is struggling for survival at the present. The recently reopened Royal Court Theatre on Sloane Square, Chelsea, is famous for drama; the Royal Shakespeare Company at the Barbican and Shakespeare's Globe Theatre on Bankside stages works by the Bard and other playwrights.

In addition to the big West End theaters there are dozens of excellent suburban playhouses, and summer outdoor theater is performed in Regent's Park and Holland Park, west of Kensington. There is also a large and proliferating number of fringe venues where you can see experimental and offbeat works for a fraction of the price of a West End theater ticket. Or you can buy same-day half price tickets (cash only) at the booth on Leicester Square (0207/836 0971).

A night at the **opera** may mean watching the English National Opera (who sing all works in English) at the Coliseum in St. Martin's Lane, or the prestigious Royal Opera Company performing in the lavishly renovated Royal Opera House in Covent Garden. This lovely stage is also home to the **Royal Ballet**. If advance bookings are sold out, one ticket per caller is on sale after 10am on the day of the performance, though be prepared for long lines. The Royal Ballet also plays under the stars in mid-summer at the open-air theater in Holland Park.

When it comes to **modern dance** you can't do better than the London Contemporary Dance Theatre, based at the Place Theatre (17 Duke's Road, WC1), or the Ballet Rambert, based at the capital's leading contemporary dance venue, Sadler's

Wells Theatre in Islington (Rosebery Ave, EC1).

Classical **concerts** take place primarily at the South Bank Arts Centre, the Barbican, and the Royal Albert Hall. Smaller, more intimate venues include Wigmore Hall (Wigmore Street, off Oxford Street), St. John's Church, Smith Square (near Westminster Abbey)

Enjoy a performance of the English National Opera at the London Coliseum.

and St. Martin-in-the-Fields in Trafalgar Square. If you are in town between mid-July and mid-September, don't miss the informal Henry Wood Promenade Concerts (the "Proms") at the Royal Albert Hall. Holders of cheap tickets (on sale one hour beforehand) sit, stand, or even walk round (hence the name, from promenade) while the music plays.

Lunchtime concerts of chamber, organ, or choral music are one of the great pleasures of everyday London culture. They usually start at 1pm, and venues include the two churches mentioned above plus many of Wren's delightful City churches. Performances are free, but do make a donation towards church maintenance. For details pick up a leaflet from the City Tourist Information Office at St. Paul's Churchyard.

Ever since the sixties, London has been the mecca for all forms of **rock and pop music,** with hundreds of bands playing in the city every week. You can nearly always catch major world acts playing in large, soulless arenas such as Wembley or Earl's Court, but smoky pubs and clubs are where you'll find the real London scene. London is also home to some excellent jazz venues. Ronnie Scott's on Frith Street in Soho is the longest-established and best of the bunch, though Soho and Covent Garden in general boast a number of good jazz clubs and restaurants where the music is as important as the food.

London's **nightclubs** are as vibrant and cosmopolitan as anywhere in the world. Some clubs have a different type of music — and crowd — every night, so read the listings magazines to make sure you know what you are going to. Dressing the part is the key to getting in: Bouncers will turn you away if you don't fit their arbitrary profile.

London's **cinema** scene is not up to American standards of recent-release choice, and tend to have a limited number of movies in play at any time. The blockbusters play in the West End, particularly on Leicester Square, but if you look around carefully,

you'll find you can catch films from every era and every part of the world.

SPORTS

The British have always been a sporty race, and Londoners are no exception. There's horse riding, inline-skating, and paddle-boating in Hyde Park, swimming in Hampstead Heath, sailing and windsurfing in Docklands, and many of London's parks (including Regent's Park) offer cheap public tennis courts. You'll find driving ranges and a few golf courses at Richmond Park.

London boasts over 43 mainstream theaters, including the Palace Theater in Soho.

Whatever sport you want to participate in, call Sportsline (Tel. 0207/222 8000) for free information.

When it comes to spectator sports, Londoners (like all Brits) are mad for **football** (soccer). Between 20,000 and 40,000 supporters turn out each Saturday to see the likes of Arsenal, Tottenham Hotspur (Spurs), or Chelsea. Look in the national papers on a Saturday morning or any of the London listings magazines to see who's playing.

The **rugby** season runs from September to April. Twickenham is the main venue for amateur Rugby Union matches (Tel. 0208/892 8161); take the train from Waterloo. The Rugby League finals take place in May at Wembley Stadium (Tel. 0208/900 1234), located conveniently at the Wembley Park tube stop. Local games are held throughout London, and are listed in the Saturday edition of all national newspapers.

Calendar of Events

January/February Jan. 1:*New Year's Day London Parade.*

February *Chinese New Year.* Chinese New Year Celebrations in Soho's Chinatown, with traditional lion dances.

March/April *Oxford versus Cambridge University Boat Race.* The mighty teams battle it out on the Thames from Putney to Mortlake, you watch from the banks (may fall in late March or early Apr.).

April Third Sun. in Apr.: *London Marathon.* The world's largest with some 30,000 runners raising £5 million for charity

May Third or fourth week in May: *Chelsea Flower Show.* The most prestigious annual gardening exhibition in the world.

June *Royal Ascot Horse Races.* Horse races where upper class shows off their new hats; *Trooping the Colour.* The Queen inspects the troops at her official birthday parade (Saturday nearest 11 June); Late June and early July: *All England Lawn Tennis Championships.* The world's greatest tennis players compete for the Wimbledon title.

July/September *Henry Wood Promenade Concerts*.* Classical music concerts for eight weeks at the Royal Albert Hall.

August Last Sun. & Mon.(usually): *Notting Hill Carnival*: Huge Caribbean street party on Portobello Road.

September: Sat. in early to mid-Sept.: *Great River Race.* Hundreds of traditional boats race from Richmond to Greenwich.

October: Sun. nearest the 21st: *Trafalgar Day Parade.* Celebrates Lord Nelson's sea victory over Napoleon.

November *State Opening of Parliament.* Watch the Queen and Royal Procession en route to re-open Parliament after the summer recess. Second Sat.: *Lord Mayor's Show.* A popular pageant of carnival floats and the newly elected Lord Mayor in procession from the Guildhall to the Law Courts, features unforgettable gilded carriage; Nov. 5: *Guy Fawkes' Day Fireworks Displays.* Bonfires and pyrotechnics lit up all over the city.

December From early Dec.: *Christmas Tree and Carols in Trafalgar Square.* Choirs sing nightly beneath the giant tree, presented every year since 1947 by the people of Oslo.

Alternatively, during the summer you can opt for a genteel game of **cricket** at Lord's (Tube: St. John's Wood; Tel. 0207/289 1611) or the Oval (Tube: Kennington; Tel. 0207/582 6660).

Tennis comes to London in a big way during the Wimbledon warm-up tournament at the Queen's Club (Tube: Baron's Court), followed by the big one at the All England Club, Wimbledon (train from Victoria to Selhurst). You can wait in line for the outside courts for the early rounds but overnight waiting is necessary for the latter stages. That is, unless, of course, you have been successful in the ticket ballot — send a stamped, self-addressed envelope to the All England Lawn Tennis Club, Church Road, Wimbledon SW19 5AE some months in advance for details; call 0208/946 2244 for more information.

Horse racing is the sport of royalty and the very rich. You can watch the thoroughbreds — often including some of the Queen's own horses — run at Ascot and Epsom, both within easy reach of London by train from Waterloo.

By contrast, **greyhound racing** is the working man's game. There are seven stadiums around London where races are held year round, including those at Wembley and Wimbledon. It's an evening event and you can combine dinner with the dogs at most tracks.

The best things in life are free — a riverfront stroll down South Bank.

EATING OUT

The days of reviling London's food and restaurants are long, long gone. The restaurant scene in this city can rival even Paris for the sheer number and variety of establishments, and the marvelous and talented new generation of chefs in the kitchen. There are Michelin stars shining over London these days, and getting a table at some of the city's best restaurants can take literally weeks (i.e., make your dinner reservations long before you leave for London). People are willing to spend their money on high quality food and good service, and restaurants are starting to catch on to the concept.

We offer a selection of recommended restaurants at the end of this guide (see page 134). The most comprehensive guide to restaurants in London is the *Time Out Guide to Eating and Drinking in London*; the *Evening Standard* also publishes a good, up-to-date restaurant guide. Restaurant Switchboard is a free service to which many London restaurateurs belong, although the advice given is claimed to be impartial. If you're stuck for an idea they will be pleased to help out and will also book you a table free of charge; Tel. 0208/888 8080.

Hours for Eating & Drinking

Breakfast is usually served from around 8am to 10:30am, and lunch is from noon to 2:30pm. Afternoon tea is served from 3 to 5pm, and dinner runs from 7 to 11pm (most Londoners dine after 8pm). In practice you can eat what you want when you want if only you know where to look in London (for odd-hour dining, Soho and Covent Garden have the most options dining round the clock).

With the liberalization of Britain's archaic licensing hours, many pubs now open all day from 11am to 11pm Monday to Saturday. Sunday hours are noon to 3pm and 7 to 10:30pm.

International Restaurants

Every significant cuisine in the world is represented in London. You can choose from Afghan to Vietnamese, with just about every shade of regional cooking in between. The top end is still dominated by the French, though home-grown chefs are making a determined assault with their own brand of "Modern British" cuisine, which is a match for any cuisine in the world. Italian food has always been very popular, and a number of restaurants are now getting well away from the old-fashioned image of lashings of pasta and oversize pepper mills.

Indian and Chinese restaurants dominate the ethnic scene, and these can be an excellent lunch-time choice with bargain, *prix-fixe* buffets. Try *dim sum* (savory dumplings) in any of Soho's Chinese restaurants during the day. The inter-

Who says you can't enjoy London sitting down? Watch the city go by from one of London's many outdoor cafés.

est in Asian food has grown so that Thai, Malaysian, and more recently Vietnamese restaurants are becoming well established in London. Middle Eastern restaurants are also popular, especially in the Arab neighborhoods around Baker Street. There aren't a huge number of vegetarian restaurants yet, but that's also changing. Try around Neal's Yard or go to any of the Crank's branches. Sushi conveyor belt restaurants, once a novelty, seem to be springing up all over.

What & Where to Eat — English Style

If you just want a native snack and you're on a limited budget, your best bet is probably a pub or wine bar. In some cases the latter are no more than restaurants with an extended wine list; the best kind, often to be found in the City, are dark and old-fashioned with sawdust on the floor, and are usually full of business types in pinstripes. The quality of pub food varies enormously, but as many establishments serve from a buffet at least you see what you are getting.

Breakfast

The full English breakfast — eggs, bacon, sausage, eggs, tomatoes, beans, toast, and perhaps mushrooms all on one plate — is quite a lot to start the day. At the better, traditional establishments kippers and porridge may also be on the menu. If this sounds a little heavy, don't worry, lighter fare is nearly always available.

Lunch

If you do choose a pub then it's always worth checking out the ploughman's lunch. This consists of bread, cheese (or ham, pâté, or sausage), salad, and pickle. If the bread is freshly-made and the cheese is a good wedge of farmhouse Cheddar or Stilton, then this can be delicious, but in many pubs, unfortunately, the standard is not high. If you cannot see what is on offer simply ask what on the menu is home-made. Scotch eggs are hard-boiled eggs wrapped in sausage meat and deep-fried, and Cornish pasties (pro-nounced *PAS-teas*) are pastries filled with a mixture of beef and vegetables. They may sound tempting but in London are invariably pre-packaged.

Hot food in pubs may include steak and kidney pie, chick-en and mushroom pie, and shepherd's pie — a casserole of minced lamb (or beef, when it may be called cottage pie), carrots, and onions, topped with mashed potatoes. On Sundays you may find pub lunches of roast lamb or beef, vegetables, and the best British food of all, Yorkshire pud-ding with gravy.

Fish and chip shops serve cod, plaice, haddock, and other types, all battered and deep fried. Look for a place with a queue that is long.

If you want a real taste of the old East End look for a Pie & Mash Shop (most close on Sunday) where you'll get minced beef pie and mashed potatoes with a unique green sauce called "liquor" that is made from parsley. Eels may also be on the menu. Not surprisingly, most of these are in the east of London. The nearest true Pie & Mash shop to the West End is Cookes at The Cut, by Waterloo Station.

Afternoon Tea

A grand old hotel is the best place for traditional afternoon tea. Tea comes with thinly sliced sandwiches (egg and watercress, smoked salmon, cucumber, or tomato); scones (similar to American biscuits, but sweeter) or crumpets (somewhat like an "English muffin"); and a selection of pastries and mini-desserts. If you order a "cream tea," your scones will be served with cream and jam (sometimes real clotted cream but more often simply whipped cream). And of course you will be offered a choice of tea, perhaps smoky Lapsang Souchong, scented Earl Grey, Assam, Darjeeling, or any one of a dozen different types.

Dinner

Starters: They may actually be hard to find, but the following are traditional starters: smoked Scottish salmon; Colchester oysters; potted shrimps cooked with butter and spices and preserved in earthenware jars; country pâtés made from chicken or pork livers.

Sandwiches, scones, and crumpets galore — afternoon tea along Shaftsbury Avenue.

Main courses: England's classic dish is roast beef and crusty Yorkshire pudding. Even the mad cow disease scare of the middle 1990s failed to slow down the national beef consumption for long. Roast leg of lamb with tangy mint sauce and roast pork with applesauce are also popular. Roasts are normally served only on a Sunday in traditional English restaurants, hotels, and some pubs. At any other time the best place in London for roasts is Simpson's-in-the-Strand (see page 137). Game, such as wild duck, pheasant, partridge, and venison, is traditionally British. Salt beef is a delicious dish that you may find in the East End.

Traditional fish dishes include turbot with lobster and shrimp sauce; baked trout with bacon; poached or grilled fresh salmon

Sample from a wide variety of traditional bitters, lagers, and continental-style brews at one of London's local pubs.

with Hollandaise sauce or made into fishcakes. Many seafood houses serve oysters, and the place to eat these in real style (and at great expense) is at the Bibendum Oyster Bar (see page 142).

Desserts

Traditional English "sweets" or "puddings" range from a light fruit "fool" (puréed fruit mixed with cream), or a syllabub (includes wine), to a heavy, rib-sticking jam roly-poly or treacle (molasses) pudding. These desserts may be flavored with jam, treacle, or fruit, then steamed. Fruit pies and crumbles, with a top crust of crumbly pastry, are old favorites. Look out, too, for sherry trifle — fruit, gelatin, and ladyfingers soaked in sherry, and topped with custard and whipped cream. The British custard is poured over crumbles and is delicious, as is the double cream that often accompanies a rich chocolate dessert.

Cheese

Don't miss the opportunity to sample a selection of English cheeses: stilton, a blue-veined cheese; cheddar, which comes in a number of varieties ranging from mild to sharp; double Gloucester, a tangy orange-red cheese; Caerphilly from Wales, a mild white crumbly cheese; and Derby, mild and creamy, particularly good with fruit. Cheese is usually eaten with cheese biscuits (crackers) rather than bread.

London's Pubs

The capital claims more than 5,000 public houses, the oldest dating back nearly 500 years, but even Victorian pubs seem laden with centuries of social history.

Beer is the traditional British drink, and when you ask for a beer in a pub you will be given the brown-colored brew known as *bitter.* The "bitter" taste comes from the addition of hops to the brew, but despite its name, many bitters are quite sweet and fruity. You no longer have to ask for "real ale" (beer made and served in the traditional way) in London as almost every pub now serves it anyway. The chilled pale drink known to Americans and Europeans as beer is *lager* to the British. Pubs often serve many different types of beer, so look at the dispensing pumps and specify the name of the beer you want to try. Or ask the bar staff for a "half" (a half-pint) of their lowest-strength bitter then work your way up to the stronger brews. If you don't like bitter, don't worry. American and Continental lagers are almost as popular as the traditional British brew in London pubs these days.

Try the following pubs for atmosphere, historical interest, good beer, and often good food.

The West End: The Grenadier, Old Barrack Yard, Wilton Row, Knightsbridge; Red Lion, Waverton Street, Mayfair;

Red Lion, Duke of York Street, St. James's (closed on Sundays); The Albert, Victoria Street (between Victoria station and Parliament Square); The French House (an oddity, try the French wine, rather than the beer!), Dean Street, Soho; The Lamb or The Sun, both on Lamb's Conduit Street, WC1; The Lamb & Flag, Rose Street, Covent Garden.

The City: Ye Olde Cock Tavern, Fleet Street; Ye Olde Cheshire Cheese, Wine Office Court off Fleet Street; The Cittie of Yorke, High Holborn; The Blackfriar, Queen Victoria Street, by Blackfriar's Bridge; The Jamaica Wine House, St. Michael's Alley, Cornhill; The Cartoonist, Shoe Lane off Chancery Lane; Ye Olde Watling by St. Paul's. (Remember that most City pubs close at weekends.)

By law, children under 14 cannot enter a pub; children over 14 must be accompanied by an adult and cannot purchase or drink alcohol. A 16-year-old may drink certain alcoholic drinks in the restaurant only, at the discretion of the landlord. The minimum age to be served alcohol is 18, though this too is at the landlord's discretion. If you have children with you it is worth seeking out pubs with gardens or family rooms (i.e., without a bar) where children are made welcome.

Late-opening bars and cafés make Covent Garden an after-theater hotspot.

Chain Restaurants

London has a lot of chains restaurants, many of which are quite good and reasonably priced. Here are just a few to look out for:

Ask Pizza & Pasta. The usual pizza, pasta, salads served quickly at a fair enough price. Nice atmosphere in most.

Calzones. Thinnest-crust pizza in town, pasta, salads and of course the eponymous pocket pizza filled with a large selection of fillings.

Café Rouge. The atmosphere at this chain of inexpensive French restaurants is Parisien, and most have outdoor tables.

Cranks. This London vegetarian mainstay is not really a restaurant, but rather a cafeteria with tables, offering excellent vegetarian fare at decent prices.

Ed's Easy Diner. Plenty of fried foods and milkshakes at this "American diner" chain, but not quite the real thing.

Patisserie Valeries. Fabulous pastries and croissants, as well as appetizing hot meals — breakfast, lunch and dinner.

Pret à Manger. Basic lunch take-away shop, although some have eat-in tables. A large selection of fresh sandwiches, salads, snacks, desserts, and drinks.

New Culture Revolution. Lots of Chinese noodle dishes, served fast and fresh.

Pizza Express. Thin-crust pizza, limited pasta choices, and good salads and desserts.

Sofra. Excellent for mixed mezza meals at this Middle Eastern chain.

Wagamama Noodle Bar. Seating is at large shared tables; it's noisy, quick and good value for money at this chain of Japanese restaurants.

HANDY TRAVEL TIPS

An A–Z Summary of Practical Information

A

ACCOMMODATIONS see also YOUTH HOSTELS.

London has a huge selection of hotels, from luxury to budget, with plenty of bed and breakfasts ("B&B") and serviced apartments available as well. All of these accommodations, even the five-star hotels charging upwards of $500 a night, are noteworthy for big prices and small rooms. The budget hotels range from spartan to abysmal; a better option for those looking to save is to check out the B&B agencies. Hotels and guesthouses are inspected and categorized according to the facilities they offer. The grades start at "listed" and go up from 1 through 5 crowns. However, this rating does not reflect the character of the establishment or the personal service that is offered there.

Any of the London Tourist Information Centres (listed on page 122) have brochures that can help you find a room. For a small fee and a deposit, these centers have a booking service that will get you a hotel. Additionally, you can book by telephone (credit cards only) through London Tourist Board's Telephone Accommodation Booking Service (Tel. 0207/604 2890). If you write to the London Tourist Board at least six weeks in advance stating your budget and requirements, a reservation can also be made. Their address: 26 Grosvenor Gardens, London SW1W 0DU.

B&B and serviced apartment agencies offer attractive accommodation in private homes in central London. Contact London First Choice Apartments, Tel. 0208-575 8877; Uptown Reservations, Tel. 0207/351 3445; or Holiday Apartments Ltd., Tel. 0207/235 2486.

Budget travelers can book a hostel at London tourist information offices. A good web site for hotel rooms is <www.London-hotel.net>.

AIRPORTS

London is served by three major airports, Heathrow, Gatwick, and Stansted. The smaller airports of Luton and City are primarily for chartered, budget, or short-hop flights.

Heathrow is located 24 km (15 miles) west of central London. The Heathrow Express is a train that goes from the airport to Paddington

London

Station in fifteen minutes, and leaves every fifteen minutes for about £10. The Piccadilly underground line provides the least expensive link to all parts of London for £3.40; it's not a good alternative during rush hours, or if you have a lot of luggage. A black taxi will take between 45 minutes and an hour to Central London for about £40 and up. The London Transport Airbus goes to King's Cross train station with several stops at hotels en route for about £7; buses depart every 20–30 minutes and the journey time is usually around one hour.

Gatwick airport lies 43 km (27 miles) south of London. The British Rail (BR) Gatwick Express leaves every 15 minutes for Victoria station and takes around 30 minutes for £10.20. The Flightline 777 or 778 to Victoria costs £8. A black taxi will cost about £70.

Stansted airport is a beautiful modern airport 54 km (34 miles) northeast of London. The Stansted Skytrain leaves for Liverpool Street station every 30 minutes between 5am and 11pm and costs £10 each way. The Flightline Coach leaves for Victoria Station, with stops along the way, every hour and costs £13 round trip, £9 one way. Taxis will cost about £50 or more.

B

BABYSITTERS

Most large hotels will be able to help you with child-care arrangements. Childminders (Tel. 0207/935 3000) is a reputable agency. Expect to pay an initial registration fee of £10 then up to £6 an hour, with a four-hour minimum, plus travel expenses. Universal Aunts (Tel. 0207/738 8937) is an organization that provides a wide range of care-giving services for both young and old.

BUDGETING FOR YOUR TRIP

To give you an idea what to expect here are some average prices in pounds sterling (£). However annual inflation and other factors can cause sudden changes, so they must be regarded as approximate.

Accommodations. For a double room with a bath in Central London, excluding breakfast, including VAT, expect to pay anywhere from £100 to over £250 per night.

Meals and drinks. For a decent English breakfast, expect to pay anywhere from £6 and up, for a Continental breakfast £3 and up; for lunch (in a pub, including one drink) expect to pay £6; for dinner (three courses, including wine, at a reasonable restaurant), expect to pay £25–30. A bottle of house wine will cost £7–10, a pint of beer £2; coffee 60p–£1.50 per cup.

Entertainment. A ticket to the cinema will cost around £8; cover at a disco or club £8–10. A walking tour costs about £5; a hop-on, hop-off bus tour of Central London costs £15 adult, £6 children; admission to museums and art galleries from £3–10 per adult, with children usually half-price, but family tickets are often available for those with several children.

Transportation. Consider that a one-day Travelcard on the Underground costs £3.40. You will spend considerably more if you use taxis or rent a car (the latter is strongly discouraged unless you are actually leaving London proper).

C

CAR RENTAL/HIRE see also DRIVING.
Heavy traffic and a lack of parking space mean that a car is more of a hindrance than a help in central London. Public transportation is quite adequate for trips to Greenwich, Windsor, Kew, and Hampton Court, so it is only advisable to rent a car if you want to explore farther afield. All the global car rental companies are represented in London; most have outlets at the major airports as well as in central London. To rent a car, you will need a valid driving license and a credit card. You must be at least 21 years old and have held a driving license for one year. The cost of renting a car from an international company with unlimited mileage, including tax and comprehensive

insurance, ranges £46 per day (£250 per week) for an economy car to £63 per day (£298 per week), for a larger car. The alternate insurance coverage that is provided by some major credit cards is not valid in the UK. Collision Damage Waiver (CDW) insurance is almost always part of the standard rates for car rental and cannot be declined by a renter. Remember that the norm in the UK is for a car without air-conditioning and with a manual transmission.

CHILDREN see also BABYSITTERS.
Check our section LONDON FOR CHILDREN (see page 69). If you run out of ideas on how to keep little ones amused, call the London Tourist Board's "What's On for Children" line for some up-to-the-minute and friendly advice (Tel. 0839/123 424, calls charged at up to 49p per minute).

CLIMATE
The best thing about visiting London is that there is really no "must go" season. Each month holds something wonderful to entertain you, even deep dark December, when the museums are so warm and inviting.

Temperatures	J	F	M	A	M	J	J	A	S	O	N	D
average daily F	43	44	50	56	62	69	71	71	65	58	50	45
maximum * C	6	7	10	13	17	20	22	22	19	14	10	7
average daily F	36	36	38	42	47	53	56	56	52	46	42	38
minimum * C	2	2	3	6	8	12	3	13	11	8	5	4

*Maximum temperatures are measured in the early afternoon, minimum temperatures before sunrise.

CLOTHING
London is best approached with layers of clothing, as the weather can change rather crazily within the course of one day. While the city's reputation for rain may be somewhat exaggerated, you should pack an umbrella. Summer has lately been developing some tropical tendencies, but you should still bring a sweater and trousers even in August. Like any great metropolitan city, casual stylishness is quite common on the street, in restaurants and cafés, and at the theater.

COMPLAINTS

If your complaint is against a tourist attraction and you can't resolve it with the manager, contact the nearest London Tourist Bureau Information Centre. If you're unhappy with a purchase, you have the right to return it as long as you have the receipt and the original packaging. If the shop refuses, or you have any other problem involving overcharging or bad workmanship, you can appeal to the Citizens Advice Bureau (CAB). Call directory assistance at 192 for the number of the local CAB office. The CAB Greater London office is at 136-144 City Road, EC1, Tel. 0207/549 0800.

CRIME & SAFETY

While London's crime rate is lower than that of most other big cities, it is rising. Women especially need to take precautions when going out: The one crime rate that is higher in London than in New York City is rape. Pickpockets still ply their trade as in Dickens's day: Hold on to your purse and put your wallet in a breast pocket in public. Be on your guard after dark away from crowded streets and in the underground. Use only legitimate minicabs and black taxis, and avoid the top deck of a night bus.

In an emergency, dial 999 from any telephone (no money or card required). Otherwise phone the nearest police station, listed under "Police" in the telephone directory.

CUSTOMS & ENTRY FORMALITIES

Citizens of Australia, Canada, New Zealand, South Africa, and the United States, as well as citizens of EU countries, need only a valid passport for tourist visits. However, travelers from some other Commonwealth countries must have a visa. Check before departure. There are no passport controls between Britain and the Republic of Ireland.

Upon arrival you will have to fill in an entry card stating the address where you will be staying. The immigration officer will stamp your passport, allowing you to stay in Britain for a specific length of time. If your plans are uncertain ask for several months so you don't have to apply for an extension later. Provided you look respectable and have sufficient funds to cover your stay there should not be a problem.

In British ports and airports, passengers with goods to declare follow the red channel; those with nothing to declare take the green route; those from an EU country go through the blue channel. You may bring in a reasonable amount of tobacco and alcohol for your personal use. If in doubt, the Foreign & Commonwealth's web site is very helpful in such matters <http://www.fco.gov.uk/travel/default.asp>.

There is no limit on how much foreign currency you may import into Britain, and the export of pounds is not restricted. Check to see whether your own country has any regulations on the import and export of currency.

D

DRIVING see also CAR HIRE.
If you are bringing in your own car or one from Europe you will need the registration papers and insurance coverage. The usual formula is the Green Card, an extension to the normal insurance, validating it for other countries.

Throughout Britain, the driver and all passengers must use seat belts. Motorcycle riders must wear a crash helmet, and a driving license is required for all types of motorcycle. Sixteen is the lower age limit for mopeds, seventeen for motorcycles and scooters. It is illegal to talk on a mobile phone while driving.

Driving conditions. Remember to drive on the left. Pay special attention at crossings (corners) and roundabouts (traffic circles). Traffic already on the roundabout has precedence over cars waiting and the rule is to give way to the right.

Driving through London is difficult even for the locals. If you must drive, get a large *London A-Z* book or map to plot your route. However, most maps will not indicate the large number of one-way streets that make navigating London quite difficult. It's a good idea to know which districts you are heading for and/or through, as these names will be likely on the signs indicating routes. It is best to take public transport into Central London.

Parking. Parking meters in central London are expensive at around £2 per hour, and the stay is often limited (cost and permitted duration indicated on meter). A yellow line means no parking, a double yellow line means no waiting, a red double line means no stopping. Parking is particularly restricted between 8:30am–6:30pm Monday–Friday and 8:30am–1:30pm Saturdays. After these times you may be able to park on single yellow lines and metered spaces free of charge, but do check. Never park in those meterless spaces marked for resident permit holders: You'll get a big fine, a wheel clamp, or towed away. For longer stays use a parking lot.

Fuel and oil. Petrol (gasoline) is now sold almost everywhere (priced in liters), and is quite expensive.

Drinking and driving. If you plan to drink more than half a pint of beer or a single measure of spirits, leave the car behind. Penalties are severe.

Road signs. Britain has adopted the same basic system of pictographs in use throughout Europe. The Highway Code is the official booklet of road usage and signs, available at most bookshops.

E

ELECTRICITY
The standard current in Britain is 240 volt, 50 cycle AC. You will need an adapter for any appliance you bring from home, as well as a converter unless the appliance is equipped with one. Many laptop computers have built-in transformer/converters, but do check to be sure. Most hotels have special sockets for shavers that operate on 240 or 110 volts.

London

Fluid measures

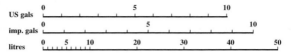

Distance

EMBASSIES & CONSULATES

All the following are in London and are open to the public Monday–Friday (visa section often open for only part of the day):

Australia: Australia House, Strand, WC2B 4LA; Tel. 0207/379 4334; open 10am–4pm.

Canada: Tourist Information, 1 Grosvenor Square, W1; Tel. 0207/887 5107; open 8–11am; High Commission; Tel. 0207/258 6600; open 9am–3pm.

Republic of Ireland: 17 Grosvenor Place, SW1X 7HR; Tel. 0207/235 2171; open 9:30am–5pm (Passport office: Tel. 0207/245 9033).

New Zealand: New Zealand House, Haymarket, SW1Y 4TQ; Tel. 0207/930 8422; passport office open10am–noon and 2–4pm; general tourist inquiries 9am–5pm.

South Africa: South Africa House, Trafalgar Square, WC2N 5DP; Tel. 0207/451-7299; open 10am–noon and 2–4pm.

US: 24 Grosvenor Square, W1A 1AE; Tel. 0207/499 9000; open 8:30am–5:30pm.

EMERGENCIES

For police, fire brigade or ambulance dial 999 from any telephone (no money or card required) and tell the operator which service you require.

ETIQUETTE

Some of the legendary characteristics of the English — their reserve and stiff-upper-lipism for example — are based in some historical truth, but these national stereotypes are becoming less common these days. While it remains true that one doesn't chat loudly on a rush-hour underground train, or elbow people aside in formal queues, the behavior and language of the local Londoner are becoming a little looser, louder, and more profane than of old. Even so, courtesy is still common, and the more you give, the more you will get. You may be addressed as Sir or Madam by a waiter, a clerk, a shop assistant, or a police officer. You may also, in some parts, be addressed as Darling, or Luv. But you mustn't return the greeting; it might be construed as sarcasm. On a first meeting use the formal address Mr. or Mrs. (Smith). You will probably soon be on first-name terms. Young people, of course, are much more relaxed and encounter few formal barriers.

G

GAY & LESBIAN TRAVELERS

The gay scene in London centers around Soho, Hampstead, Clapham, and Earl's Court, with Old Compton Street in Soho offering specialist bookstores, bars, and shops as well as a hair salon, a travel agency, and a taxi company. There are also excellent gay nightclubs that heteros love too, such as Heaven. For advice and information call the Lesbian and Gay Switchboard at 0207/837 7324. Find listings for gay venues in *Time Out*.

GETTING TO LONDON

By Air. From North America, there are direct flights from Atlanta, Boston, Chicago, Dallas/Fort Worth, Los Angeles, Montreal, New York, Newark, San Francisco, Toronto, and other cities. From Australia and New Zealand, there are several weekly flights from Sydney, Melbourne, Perth, and Auckland to London with stops en route. From South Africa, there are daily flights from Johannesburg and Cape Town.

London

By Sea. Ferries link Britain with many ports on the Continent. The two major lines are P&O and Sealink Stena Line, which operate several crossings between the major channel ports. The fastest crossing of the English Channel is aboard the Hoverspeed hovercraft, which makes the Dover–Calais and Dover–Boulogne trip in just 35 minutes. Fast trains link most of these ports to London. The principal port, Dover, is on the main British Rail Intercity network, just over 90 minutes from London. Le Shuttle service provides transport for private cars from Folkestone in Kent to Calais in France (Tel. 0990/353 535).

By Rail. The Channel Tunnel provides a direct rail link between Britain and mainland Europe. Eurostar operates regular, rapid services between London Waterloo and Paris Gare du Nord, Lille, or Brussels, with a travel time of around three hours (Tel. 01233/617 575).

GUIDES & TOURS

Get off to the right start with an introductory panoramic tour of the city. London Coaches runs the Original London Sightseeing Tour offering 90 minutes of the best of the central area with live commentary in English or taped commentary in eight other major languages. Take advantage of the hop-on, hop-off service, with stops at 30 different places; (Tel. 0207/828 6449 for more details). Tours depart regularly from the main attractions around London. Buy a ticket and pick up the bus at a nearby stop; an early start in the day is recommended.

A dozen different companies organize walking tours of the city, with themes. Some companies offer guided pub walks that are usually general area tours with some historic pubs thrown in. *What's On* and *Time Out* list times and meeting places for many of these. Recommended operators are The Original London Walks (Tel. 0207/624 3978), Historical Walks of London (Tel. 0208/668 4019), and Footsteps, which leads multilingual tours (Tel. 0162/275 4451).

There are regular river boat departures from Westminster Pier and Charing Cross Pier down to Greenwich; Tel. 0207/930 9033 or 0207/839 3572 for details. Three companies run canal cruises between Little Venice (near the Warwick Avenue/Camden Town underground stations) and Camden Lock from Easter to October: Jason's Trip (Tel. 0207/286 6752); Jenny Wren (Tel. 0207/485 4433); the London Waterbus Company (tel. 0207/482 2550). The tourist board also has a River Trips Information Line (Tel. 0839/123 432).

H

HEALTH & MEDICAL CARE

Although the National Health Service takes care of anyone in need of urgent attention free of charge, visitors from countries outside the EU have to pay for non-emergency treatment. Medical insurance is therefore strongly recommended. Your travel agent will be able to help you with a modestly priced policy. If you are taken ill you must first see a general practitioner (GP), whose task it is to diagnose and treat or, if necessary, to direct you to a specialist or hospital.

In case of emergency only, dial 999 for an ambulance. If you are ill outside normal consulting hours but your situation is not an emergency, there are 24-hour walk-in emergency rooms at the following central London hospitals:

St. Thomas's, Lambeth Palace Road (Tel. 0207/928 9292); University College, Gower Street, entrance on Grafton Way (Tel. 0207/387 9300); Chelsea and Westminster, 369 Fulham Road, SW1 (Tel. 0208/746 8000). Eye emergencies should go to Moorfields Eye Hospital, City Road (Tel. 0207/253 3411).

Late-night-opening chemists (also called pharmacies but rarely drug stores) include: Bliss, 5 Marble Arch, 9am–midnight, daily, Tel. 0207/723 6116; Boots, 44–46 Regent Street, 8:30am–8pm Mon–Fri, 9am–6pm Sat, noon–6pm Sun (Tel. 0207/734 6126); Boots, 75 Queensway, 9am–10pm Mon–Sat (Tel. 0207/229 9266).

HOLIDAYS

These are also known as bank holidays. Banks and offices are shut, but most forms of entertainment are open, on New Year's Day, Good Friday, Easter Monday, May Day (first Monday in May), Spring Bank Holiday (last Monday in May), Summer Bank Holiday (last

London

Monday in August), Christmas Day, and Boxing Day (26 December). If any of these holidays falls on a weekend, it is taken on the following Monday.

 L

LANGUAGE

You may not catch the quick, slick Cockney of a London cabbie, but then neither does the average person born beyond the sound of Bow Bells. The thick Northern accent can also be incomprehensible to English speakers from other lands. But it is the actual vocabulary that can be the most bewildering for the Transatlantics. Here is an excerpt of some more common words:

British	American	British	American
bill	check (restaurant)	**queue**	v. stand in line;
bonnet	hood (of car)		n. line
boot	trunk (of car)	**return**	round-trip (ticket)
chemist	druggist	**single**	one-way (ticket)
first floor	second floor	**tube or**	subway train
nappy	diaper	**underground**	
off-licence	liquor store		

LOST PROPERTY

If you want to claim the loss of any item on your insurance policy you must report it to the police, who will issue you with a form. If the item was on a bus or on the underground, go in person to the London Transport Lost Property Office, 200 Baker St., NW1 5RW, open 9:30am–2pm Mon–Fri.

If you were in a black taxi, contact the Metropolitan Police Lost Property Office, 15, Penton St., N1 9PU; Tel. 0207/833 0996.

M

MEDIA

Most newsstands carry copies of the *International Herald Tribune,* and American magazines are also widely available. However, periodicals from further afield in the English-speaking world are rare.

To find out what's happening in London in the fields of arts, entertainment, sports, and nightlife buy one of the weekly listings magazines — *What's On* or *Time Out* are the most popular. The daily *London Evening Standard* is also a good source of information, especially the Hot Tickets supplement on Thursdays.

Standard TVs pick up two BBC channels and two independent channels. Satellite dishes or special cables are needed to pick up other stations.

The BBC World Service (648 KHz/463 m) provides the most comprehensive international news coverage.

MONEY

Currency. The monetary unit is the pound sterling (£), divided into 100 pence (p). Banknotes: £5, £10, £20, £50. Coins: 1p, 2p, 5p, 10p, 20p, 50p, £1, £2.

Currency Exchange. The leading banks have "High Street branches" in all major shopping streets in London, including the suburbs. Many neighborhood banks will be able to change your foreign currency or traveler's checks (look for the "Foreign Exchange" sign). Private currency exchange offices are known as Bureaux de Change.

If you are exchanging a reasonable amount of money, shop around. Rates can vary considerably, and bureaux de change in particular charge heavily for their handy locations and the convenience of late opening. If you do use one of these, make sure they are displaying an LVCB sticker or plaque.

You will probably get the best rate by using an ATM, known here as Cashpoints, with your bank card from home. There are hundreds of cash machines all over London, operating on global systems, such as

London

Cirrus, Mac, and others. *A word of caution:* The machines here require a limit of four numbers for a PIN, so you may have to change yours before leaving. Also, if your PIN is a word, memorize the numbers, because there aren't always letters on the key pads here.

Credit Cards and Traveler's Checks. Credit cards are widely accepted in hotels, restaurants, and shops, but traveler's checks are not. Change them in a bank or a bureau de change (same rules as for cash, see above). You will need your passport as proof of identity.

Tax Refunds for Tourists. A sales tax called Value Added Tax (VAT), currently 17.5%, is levied on most shop goods in Britain. VAT is almost always included in the price displayed in store; where it is not, it will usually say the price "plus VAT." Most big shops that have significant tourist trade participate in a scheme whereby non-EU travelers are refunded the VAT paid on goods less a small service charge. Participating shops usually display a "tax-free shopping" sticker. Your refund will rarely be even close to the original 17.5%, but for costly items, it may be worth applying for. There is usually a minimum purchase price of £100 and you must leave the country within three months to qualify. Ask the shop to issue you with the appropriate form. This should be presented with the goods for validation to the customs officer at the airport or seaport of departure. A separate form is issued for larger goods that have to go into the cargo hold. There are Cashback desks at the airport which will issue you a refund on the spot of about 5% of the VAT paid. Some refunds are done by check to the home address, which takes as many as 12 weeks to process and receive. For further information on VAT refunds contact the Shopping Advisory Service in the British Travel Centre on Regent Street.

OPEN HOURS
Banks: Usually Mon–Fri 9:30am–3:30pm. Some banks open for limited services on Saturday mornings.

Museums: Mon–Sat 10am–5 or 6pm, and Sun from 2 or 2:30–5 or 6pm. Some museums open earlier on Sundays; some open later on Mondays; some also offer late-night viewing once a week.

Offices: Mon–Fri 9 or 9:30am–5 or 5:30pm.

Pubs: Traditional hours Mon–Sat 11am–3pm and 5:30–11pm, Sun noon–2pm and 7–10:30pm; extended hours Mon–Sat 11am–11pm, Sun noon–3pm and 7–10:30pm.

Shops: Mon–Sat 9 or 9:30am–5:30 or 6pm. Some shops open Sun noon–5pm. Late-night shopping nights are Wed till 7pm in Chelsea and Knightsbridge, Thurs till 7:30 or 8pm in Oxford and Regent Streets.

PHOTOGRAPHY & VIDEO
Film is widely available, and there are plenty of one-hour and 24-hour outfits in Central London where you can have your film developed. Videotapes sold in the UK, however, may not be compatible with your machine at home; if you are not sure, ask before you buy.

POLICE
London police are usually unarmed and, on the whole, they are friendly and helpful. Do not expect leniency if you break the law, however, and don't expect that the accused has the same rights in the UK as they do in other countries. For emergencies telephone 999.

POST OFFICES
Post offices are generally open Mon–Fri 9am–5:30 or 6pm, and Sat 9am–noon or 12:30pm. Provincial and suburban offices may close for lunch. The post office at 24–28 William IV Street (just off Trafalgar Square) is open Mon–Sat 8am–8pm. An overseas letter costs 64p, an overseas postcard costs 38p.

London

Stamps are sold at post office counters and from vending machines outside post offices. They are also now sold in a variety of other shops (newsagents, etc.), often indicated by a red "stamps" sign.

PUBLIC TRANSPORTATION see also TAXIS

Buses. Although the red double-decker bus isn't the quickest way to get around, riding on the top deck is a great way to admire the streets and sights of London. There are two types of bus signs: A red symbol on a white background indicates a compulsory stop (unless the bus is full); a white symbol on a red background indicates a request stop where you have to wave down the bus. You will also have to ring the bell in advance of your stop to let the driver know you want to get off. If your bus is the old-fashioned type, known as a Routemaster, with an open rear platform just climb aboard and the conductor will come around and collect your fare en route. On other buses you have to pay the driver as you board, so always have some change handy to avoid delay, although they do not require exact change. Single-deck buses do short hops through the city, and there are single-decker Green Line buses serving the suburbs and outskirts.

Most buses run from about 6am–11 or 11:30pm; night buses then take over running an hourly skeleton service. Night buses charge slightly more than the day buses, and don't accept some Travelcards, so have change on hand. Fares are between 70p and £1.

Underground. The "tube" is usually the fastest way to get around London. The map is easily understood, and when in doubt, ask. Always check the front of the train to make sure that it is heading toward your destination: Many lines split into two different directions, so be alert. Buy your ticket in the station entrance hall. On your way to the platform you put it into an automatic turnstile device, which opens to let you through, and returns your ticket — don't forget to take it back! You will then feed it into the machine as you leave the station at your destination.

Trains run from around Mon–Sat 5:30am–midnight, Sun 7am–11pm. Smoking is strictly prohibited on any part of the underground. A single central zone fare is £1.50 and must be used on the *day of purchase only* (you can buy a Carnet of single-use tickets, which is ten Zone 1 tickets for only £11, and you can use the tickets for a year); the most expensive single fare is £3.50 (this is what the trip from Heathrow into Central London costs).

There is a telephone travel information service for the Underground at 0207/222 1234.

Trains. The principle mainline (as opposed to underground) stations are Euston, King's Cross, Liverpool Street, Paddington, St. Pancras, Victoria, and Waterloo. They are all connected to the underground.

Several discount passes for train travel are available. If you intend travelling around the country, consider the BritRail Pass, which allows unlimited travel for certain periods (sold outside Britain only). Ask at any mainline station for more information.

Docklands Light Railway (DLR). Service starts underground at Bank or above ground at Tower Gateway (adjacent to Tower Hill underground station) and runs east on an elevated track. Take the line to Island Gardens and get off here and walk under the Thames foot tunnel to Greenwich. With the new extension of the Jubilee Line, Docklands is on its way to becoming a developed tourist area. There are information centers at Tower Gateway and Island Gardens. Trains run Mon–Fri 5:30am–12:30am For more information on the DLR; Tel. 0207/538 9400.

Transit Passes. There are various types of Travelcards that allow unlimited travel on bus, underground and British Rail lines for various time periods. A one-day Travelcard costs £3.90 for zones 1 & 2; a weekend Travelcard costs £5.80 for zones 1 & 2. The London Visitor Travelcard is available only outside Britain through British Rail offices (with a hefty surcharge) and travel agents, and offers more or less unlimited travel for three, four, or seven days, but it is prohibitively expensive. A bus pass or Travelcard for a week or more requires a passport-size photo, and can be had from any Underground Station, newsagent, or London Travel Information Centre.

TAXIS

London's black cabs (which now can be any color and are often covered in advertising) are rated the best in the world. They are spacious inside with good window views. The drivers have passed an extremely rigorous memory test, known as "The Knowledge," which includes learning by heart over 620 routes within a 9.6 km-(6-mile) radius of Charing Cross. A taxi can be hailed on the street whenever its "For Hire" light is on. As long as the journey is under 6 miles (9.6 km) and wholly within the Metropolitan Police District, the driver is obliged to take you and the fare payable is shown on the meter.. Outside these restrictions the fare is negotiable and should be agreed beforehand. The exceptions are the airport routes, London–Heathrow, and London–Gatwick, which are metered.

Taxi fares start automatically at £1.40, which is the minimum charge for the first 873 yards or 3 minutes. (An additional £2.80 is charged if the taxi has been booked by phone.) The fare is then 84p per km (£1.40 per mile) thereafter. Surcharges are as follows: 50p per additional passenger; 10p per piece of luggage stored next to the driver; 50p Mon–Fri 8pm–midnight and Sat 6am–8pm; 60p Mon–Fri midnight–6am and 8pm Sat–6am Mon as well as all public holidays.

Black cabs can be ordered by telephone 24 hours a day (with a £2.80 pickup surcharge); Tel. 0207/286 0286; 0207/272 0272; 0207/253 5000.

Minicabs. Other taxis operating in London are known as minicabs. Minicab drivers need no special qualifications and cars are generally not metered. By law they cannot be hailed in the street nor can they solicit trade. Never accept a lift from minicab drivers offering their services at the airport or station. If you want the number of a reputable local company your hotel should be able to help you.

A tip of 10 per cent is customary.

TELEPHONES

The old familiar red boxes are now mostly gone, replaced by cubicles provided by British Telecom (BT) or Mercury. All include easy-to-understand instructions.

Coin-operated payphones take 10p, 20p, 50p, and £1 coins. Calls may be dialed direct anywhere in the world.

Phonecards can be bought from post offices or most newsagents in various denominations and eliminate the need for small change. Some BT and all Mercury phones also accept major credit cards.

Hotel telephone surcharges can be murderous, you may be better off in a telephone booth.

The prefix 0171, is in the process of being replaced with the prefix 0207, and indicates that a number is within central London; 0181, soon to be 0208, is Greater London (though this may only be a few miles from the center).

Useful numbers. Call the operator on 100 for general inland/domestic queries or if you are having difficulties getting through. Directory Inquiries: 192. International Directory Inquiries: 153. International Operator: 155.

TIME ZONES

In winter Great Britain is on Greenwich Mean Time. In summer (April–October) clocks are put forward one hour.

Summer time differences:

New York	London	Jo'burg	Sydney	Auckland
7 am	noon	1 pm	9 pm	11 pm

TIPPING

Restaurants may add a service charge to your bill, in which case the tip is included. If you do not feel the service warranted the charge you may deduct part or all of it, though you will have to justify this. In the UK, while it has not historically been customary to tip barstaff, it is becoming more common. Never feel obliged to tip if the service has been no more than adequate. In general, you should tip waiters (10–15%, if service is not included), taxi drivers (10-15%, 50p minimum), tour guides and baggage handlers (a pound or two).

TOILETS

These may be marked in railway stations, parks and museums, as "Public Conveniences" or "WC." If you are asking for directions, simply ask for the toilets. Keep a 20p piece handy for the free-standing public toilets.

TOURIST INFORMATION

The British Tourist Authority will provide you with information before you leave home:

Australia: 210 Clarence Street, Sydney, New South Wales 2000; Tel. (2) 267-4442

Canada: Suite 600, 111 Avenue Road, Suite 450, Toronto, Ontario M5R 3J8; Tel. (416) 925-6326

South Africa: Lancaster Gate, Hyde Park Lane, Hyde Park, Sandton 2196; Tel (11) 325-0343

US: Suite 1510, 625 North Michigan Avenue, Chicago, IL 60611 (Tel. 312/787-0490).

Suite 450, World Trade Center, 350 South Figueroa Street, Los Angeles, CA 900207 (Tel. 213/628-3525).

551 Fifth Avenue, New York, NY 10176-0799 (Tel. 212/986-2200 or 800/GO-2-BRITAIN).

The London Tourist Board and Convention Bureau is the official body concerned with tourism in London. Write for information to: 26 Grosvenor Gardens, London SW1W 0DU.

In London the central tourist information offices are at Victoria Station forecourt; Selfridges, Oxford Street (basement); Liverpool Street underground station; Heathrow Terminals 1,2,3 underground station. All are open daily. The British Travel Centre, 12 Regent Street, deals with all areas of Britain and is useful for sorting out travel arrangements.

The London Tourist Board telephone information service gives information on London; Tel. 0839/123 456. You can get a touch-tone menu of the following info, or you can dial 0839-123 plus the following last three digits for specific information. 400: what's on this week; 403: current exhibitions; 411:Changing of the Guard; 416: West End shows; 424: children; 480: attractions; 481: palaces; 429: museums; 431: tours and walks; 432: river cruises.

TRAVELERS WITH DISABILITIES

The definitive guide book is Nicholson's *Access in London,* available in some bookshops (all good bookshops will order you a copy, quote ISBN 0-9485-7638-3). The LTB also provides a free leaflet, "London For All," available from Information Centres. Artsline is a free telephone information service for disabled people in London, covering the arts and entertainment (Tel. 0207/388 2227) available Mon–Fri 9:30am–5:30pm.

For details on public transport pick up "Access to the Underground," free from Tourist Information Centres or by post from London Regional Transport, Unit for Disabled Passengers, 55 Broadway, London SW1; Tel. 0207/918 3312.

The Holiday Care Service produces a brochure "Accessible Accommodation in London," available from Tourist Information Centres or from Holiday Care Service, 2 Old Bank Chambers, Station Road, Horley, Surrey RH6 9HW; Tel. 01293/774 535.

W

WEB SITES

There are a number of good general-information London sites that can help you with accommodation, tourist information, and entertainment guides. The best are:

London

<www.LondonTown.com>
<www.london-calling.co.uk>
<www.timeout.co.uk>.

WEIGHTS & MEASURES

Length

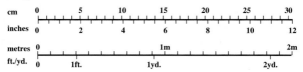

Weight

Temperature

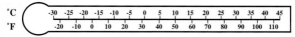

YOUTH HOSTELS & YMCAS

There are seven youth hostels in central London including interesting accommodation in the old St. Paul's choir school building in the City and a Jacobean mansion in Holland Park. Other locations are Earl's Court, Highgate, Hampstead, Oxford Street and Rotherhithe (Docklands). You must be a member to stay in one of these but joining is inexpensive and so are room rates which are around £19–22 per night for dormitory accommodation, including breakfast. You will have to book two or three months in advance; Tel. 0207/373 3400 for details.

There are also 18 YMCA hotels around London, call the National Council for YMCAs; Tel: 0208/520 5599.

Recommended Hotels

There are about 2000 hotels in London, and they run the usual gamut from disgusting to divine, with prices to match. We have tried here to take some of the gamble out of choosing a hotel, though even past experience or expert advice is no proof against establishments changing hands, neighborhoods going through transition, prices skyrocketing, or renovations that diminish the size and charm of a room.

In London there are hotel booking facilities at the main tourist information offices (see "Accommodations," page 103, and "Tourist Information," page 122). In this section we list some tried and trusted hotels to get you started.

The symbols below are a guide to the price of a standard double room with private bath. Breakfast is usually extra. Where "B&B" (bed and breakfast) is stated the price includes accommodation and breakfast. All prices are inclusive of service and tax.

$$$$	Luxury (above £200)
$$$	Expensive (£150–200)
$$	Moderate (£75–150)
$	Budget (below £75)

Unless otherwise indicated, all hotels take major credit cards (Mastercard, Visa, American Express).

Bayswater

Thistle Hyde Park $$$$ *90–92 Lancaster Gate, W2 3NR; Tel. 0207/262 2711; fax 0207/262 2147.* This Thistle establishment (formerly White's Hotel) offers all the services and amenities you could want, plus views of Hyde Park and Kensington Gardens. 193 rooms.

London

Mornington $$ *12 Lancaster Gate, W2 3LG; Tel. 0207/262 7361; fax 0207/706 1028.* Bed and breakfast in a Victorian town house with a homey atmosphere. B&B. 68 rooms.

Bloomsbury

Academy $$–$$$ *17–21 Gower St., WC1E 6HG; Tel. 0207/631 4115; fax 0207/636 3442.* Elegant Georgian terraced house with high standards of service and comfort that is also relatively affordable. 36 rooms.

Bedford $$ *83 Southampton Row, WC1 B3LB; Tel. 0207/636 7822.* Refurbished hotel with good facilities and a lovely little garden. Situated near the City and the British Museum. B&B. 184 rooms.

Grange White Hall Hotel $$$ *2–5 Montague St., WC1 B5BP; Tel. 0207/580 2224, fax 0207/580 5554.* Cozy, traditional Georgian terraced house in the shadow of the British Museum. There is a charming garden out back and two restaurants. Although the rooms are small, they are attractive. 74 rooms.

Hotel Russell $$$ *Russell Square, WC1 N1LN; Tel. 0207/837 6470; fax 0207/837 2857.* A grand old Victorian hotel that offers the tourist a fairly good deal and has all the amenities a business person could require. Some of the rooms are surprisingly spacious, and it's right on lovely Russell Square. Traditionally furnished bedrooms. 326 rooms.

Chelsea

Cadogan $$$ *75 Sloane St., SW1 X9SG; Tel. 0207/235 7141; fax 0207/245 0994.* Famous for being the hotel where Oscar Wilde was arrested. Part of the building is the former home of actress Lillie Langtry. It's beautifully decorated in the Victorian style, with all conveniences and comforts. Guests have access to gardens and tennis courts across the street. 65 rooms.

Eleven Cadogan Gardens $$$$ *11 Cadogan Gardens, Sloane Square, SW3 2RJ; Tel. 0207/730 7000; fax 0207/730 5217.* A quiet hotel with a clubby atmosphere that has been going strong for 40 years, this 1860s house is filled with antiques, leaded windows, and oak paneling. Unusual for a townhouse hotel, it has a decent exercise room. 62 rooms.

Willett $$ *32 Sloane Gardens, Sloane Square, SW1 W8DJ; Tel. 0207/824 8415; fax 0207/730 4830.* Well-equipped and nicely decorated bedrooms in a smart Chelsea town house at the foot of the King's Road. Good value for money. 18 rooms.

Covent Garden

Covent Garden Hotel $$$–$$$$ *10 Monmouth St., WC2H 9HB; Tel. 0207/806 1000; fax 0207/806 1100.* Located in the heart of Soho, this hotel is long on service and style, with an elegant sitting room, restaurant, superbly decorated rooms (of a decent size) with all expected modern conveniences, plus cell phone for rent. Popular with the young celebs. 50 rooms.

Fielding $$–$$$ *4 Broad Court, Bow Street, WC2B 5Q2; Tel. 0207/836 8305; fax 0207/497 0064.* A small, friendly hotel excellently situated for Covent Garden and the West End. Although quite, simple, and unremarkable inside, the exterior is charming. 26 rooms and 2 suites.

Savoy $$$$ *The Strand, WC2R OEU; Tel. 0207/836 4343; fax 0207/240 6040.* A hotel for the rich and famous, the Savoy is a London legend. It's an easy walk to the Thames, the National Gallery, or Covent Garden. The Savoy Hotel Grill Room is first-rate, serving classic French and English cuisine. 202 rooms.

Kensington & Holland Park

DeVere Park $ *60 Hyde Park Gate, Kensington, W8 5AS; Tel. 0207/584 0051; fax 0207/823 8583.* Comfortable, reasonably priced hotel directly across the street from Kensington Palace. It has a brasserie that is bright and cheerful, as are the very simple rooms. 93 rooms.

Halcyon $$$$ *81 Holland Park, W11 3R2; Tel. 0207/727 7288; fax 0207/229 8516.* Tastefully decorated rooms in an attractive Victorian townhouse with country-house atmosphere and antique furnishings. Given the easy walking distance to the magnificent Holland Park, this hotel has become a celebrity magnet. Friendly, courteous staff. 43 rooms.

Forte Posthouse Kensington $$–$$$ *Wright's Lane, W8 55P; Tel. 0207/937 8170; fax 0207/937 8289.* A modern hotel with a gym, indoor pool, sauna, sunbeds, squash courts, and water garden. The Forte Group pride themselves on the various deals they offer, but even the rack rate gives good value. 543 rooms.

Milestone $$$–$$$$ *1 Kensington Court, W8 5DL; Tel. 0207/917 1000; fax 0207/917 1010.* Directly across the street from Kensington Palace, this attractive hotel is great for park lovers. They feature all the conveniences and comforts to please tourists and business people alike, as well as a specially designed room for disabled guests. Charming lounge and restaurant, small health club. 62 rooms.

Knightsbridge & Belgravia

Basil Street $$$ *8 Basil Street, SW 1AH; Tel. 0207/581 3311; fax 0207/581 3693.* Known and loved by the cognoscenti, the Basil Street has charm, character, and a wonderfully traditional style. The rooms are fairly spacious, and there are beautiful antiques and art in the common areas to delight the eye. One of London's best places for afternoon tea. Excellent restaurant. 93 rooms.

Capital $$$–$$$$ *22–4 Basil St., SW3 1AT; Tel. 0207/589 5171; fax 0207/225 0011.* This is quite a sumptuous hotel, small and quiet with one of London's best restaurants. Around the corner from Harrods and the designer shops of Sloane Street. 48 rooms.

Claverly $$–$$$ *13–14 Beaufort Gardens, SW3 1PS; Tel. 0207/589 8541; fax 0207/584 3410.* An excellent deal can be had at this award-winning B&B, not the least of which is the hearty breakfast, which is included in the room rate. Rooms are individually decorated, some quite nicely, and the Knightsbridge location is convenient to all public transportation, museums, and shops. No smoking allowed in any of the rooms. 31 rooms.

Franklin $$$$ *28 Egerton Gardens, SW3 2DB; Tel. 0207/584 5533; fax 0207/584 5449.* Small, popular gem of a hotel, decorated with elegance and looking out onto a gorgeous garden. Excellent, central location, yet quiet. Great sitting rooms. 47 rooms.

Hyde Park $$$$ *66 Knightsbridge, SW1Y 7LA; Tel. 0207/235 2000; fax 0207/235 7022.* Grand old Edwardian hotel overlooking Hyde Park. Rooms recently redecorated, many with antique furnishings. Dining room has splendid views of the park. 130 rooms.

Parkes $$–$$$$ *41 Beaufort Gardens, Knightsbridge SW3 1PW; Tel. 0207/581 9944; fax 0207/581 1999.* Set in a quiet street by Harrods, the Parkes specializes in affordable suites with kitchenettes, although they also have some small, standard double rooms. The junior suites have one bedroom and a good-sized sitting room. There is a lovely dining room that serves breakfast for £5, a good deal in this neighborhood. 33 rooms.

London

Marylebone & Regent's Park

Colonnade $$ *2 Warrington Crescent, W9 1ER; Tel. 0207/286 1052; fax 0207/286 1057.* Two converted Victorian houses boasting an excellent standard of accommodation; good breakfasts and pleasant patio area. 49 rooms.

Dorset Square Hotel $$$ *39–40 Dorset Square, NW1 6QN; Tel. 0207/723 7874; fax 0171724 3328.* Elegant townhouse hotel on Dorset Square, with English country-house atmosphere and antique furnishings. Good service and all the modern conveniences. 37 rooms.

Mayfair & Piccadilly

Brown's $$$$ *29–34 Albermarle St., W1A 45W; Tel. 0207/493 6020; fax 0207/493 9381.* Small, traditional hotel, famous for its afternoon tea. First-class service and comfort, although beware of the lack of air-conditioning in summer months. 120 rooms.

Claridge's $$$$ *Brook St., W1A 2JQ; Tel. 0207/629 8860; fax 0207/499 2210.* The ultimate in luxury and discreet service, with spacious, art deco rooms and an excellent lounge for tea or cocktails. A long tradition of popularity among the elite. 189 rooms.

Connaught $$$$ *16 Carlos Place, W1Y 6AL; Tel. 0207/499 7070, fax 0207/495 3262.* Splendidly decorated rooms, faultless service and one of London's top restaurants in a charming neighborhood in the heart of Mayfair. A bit on the old-fashioned side for the business person, but heaven for tourists. 90 rooms.

Dukes $$$–$$$$ *35 St. James's Place, SW1A 1NY; Tel. 0207/491 4840; fax 0207/493 1264.* Small, elegant Edwardian hotel tucked away in a courtyard where there are gas street lamps lit each night. The prices are high, but the service is first rate, the rooms are quite spacious, and the neighborhood is gorgeous. 64 rooms.

Ritz $$$$ *150 Piccadilly, W1V 9DG; Tel. 0207/493 8181; fax 0207/493 2687.* A byword for style and elegance, with beautiful public rooms. Some rooms overlook Green Park. Afternoon tea in The Palm Court is a must, but you need to book in advance. 131 rooms.

Notting Hill Gate

Abbey Court $$–$$$ *20 Pembridge Gardens W2 4DU; Tel. 0207/221 7518; fax 0207/792 0858.* Within easy walking distance of Portobello Road, this charming town house is filled with beautiful antiques. Breakfast room and a tiny outdoor patio. No elevator. 22 rooms.

Pembridge Court $$–$$$ *34 Pembridge Gardens, W2 4DX; Tel. 0207/229 9977; fax 0207/727 4982.* Small 19th-century townhouse near Portobello Road that features its own resident cats. Decorated pleasingly with framed antique clothing accessories, and has a guest-only bar/restaurant in the basement. 20 rooms.

Portobello $$$–$$$$ *22 Stanley Gardens, W11 2NG; Tel. 0207/727 2777; fax 0207/792 9641.* Terraced house, decorated in a wildly innovative style — see the round bed and antique copper tub in the room overlooking the garden. Popular with actors, musicians, and models. 25 rooms.

Oxford Street & Baker Street

Bickenhall $–$$ *119 Gloucester Place, W1H 3PJ; Tel. 0207/935 3401; fax 0207/224 0614.* Elegant Georgian house with a pleasant patio area. 23 rooms.

Durrant's $$–$$$ *2–32 George Street, W1H 6BJ; Tel. 0207/935 8131; fax 0207/487 3510.* An excellent hotel converted from a terrace of Georgian town houses, it maintains a traditional but cozy atmosphere. It's good value, with decent sized rooms and a good location — not only near Oxford street and Regent's Park, but also across the street from the Wallace Collection. 96 rooms.

South Kensington

Blakes $$$$ *33 Roland Gardens, SW7; Tel. 0207/370 6701, fax 0207/373 0442.* Gorgeous and stylish hotel in quiet neighborhood. The rooms are all individually, exquisitely decorated, and service is superb and discreet. 51 rooms.

Gore $$$–$$$$ *189 Queen's Gate, SW7 5EX; Tel. 0207/584 6601; fax 0207/589 8127.* You are stepping into the past in this quiet hotel next to Hyde Park: The antiques and decoration of the Gore are fantastically authentic. There are two restaurants, a café, and a fine dining room. 53 rooms.

Number Sixteen $$–$$$ *16 Sumner Place, SW7 3EG; Tel. 0207/589 5232; fax 0207/584 8615.* Attractively furnished Victorian townhouse with a small garden and conservatory right off the main street of South Kensington. Many good restaurants within walking distance. B&B. 36 rooms.

Pelham $$$–$$$$ *15 Cromwell Place SW7 2LA; Tel. 0207/589 8288; fax 0207/584 8444.* Well-situated in the heart of South Kensington, the Pelham is a charmingly decorated hotel with very high standards of comfort, amenities, and service. It has an excellent restaurant. 50 rooms.

Rembrandt $$$ *11 Thurloe Place, SW7 2RS; Tel. 0207/589 8100; Fax 0207/225 3363.* Directly across the street from the Victoria & Albert Museum, this popular hotel has a pleasant sitting area, clean, comfortable rooms, all the usual hotel amenities, plus use of a health club with pool. Only executive rooms are air-conditioned. 195 rooms.

Victoria

Goring $$$–$$$$ *15 Beeston Place, Grosvenor Gardens, SW1W DJW; Tel. 0207/396-9000; fax 0207/834 4393.* Family-owned since 1910, with a persuasive claim to be London's best small hotel. Quiet location with stunning garden, and Victoria Station is conveniently located a short walk away. 79 rooms.

Hamilton House $ *60 Warwick Way, SW1V 1SA; Tel. 0207/821 7113; fax 0207/630 0806.* Small hotel conveniently located for the West End. Noisy in the front but with clean rooms and a big breakfast. B&B. 37 rooms. Mastercard and Visa only.

Oxford House $ *92–94 Cambridge St., SW1V 4Q8; Tel. 0207/834 6467; fax 0207/834 0225.* Friendly, comfortable, family-run accommodation in a 150-year-old terraced house. Quiet street. B&B. 17 rooms. Mastercard or Visa only, with 5% surcharge.

Thistle Victoria $$$ *101 Buckingham Palace Road, SW1W 03J; Tel. 0207/834 9494, fax 0207/630 1978.* Grand old Victorian hotel with large, traditionally decorated rooms right beside the Victoria train station. The lobby and sitting areas are magnificent. 366 rooms.

Wilbraham $$ *1–5 Wilbraham Place, SW1 X9AE; Tel. 0207/730 8296; fax 0207/730 6815.* Imaginatively and elegantly decorated hotel occupying three Victorian houses. Meals are served here. 64 rooms. Cash or traveler's checks only; no credit cards.

Windermere $$ *142–44 Warwick Way, SW1V 4JE; Tel. 0207/834 5163, fax 0207/630 8831.* Comfortable and simply furnished accommodation in two charming early Victorian houses close to the station. Friendly service, dining room for guests only. B&B. 18 rooms.

Recommended Restaurants

Restaurants are listed alphabetically according to location. Prices quoted are per person and include starter, mid-priced main course and dessert, but not wine, coffee, or service. A cheaper fixed-price menu is usually on offer at lunchtimes at the more expensive establishments.

In the price categories below, if a range is indicated (e.g., **$–$$**), it is meant to show that there is a clear price distinction between lunch and dinner or that the restaurant has two very different dining areas. When a London restaurant is "unlicensed," you may take along your own wine, though the restaurant may charge a corkage fee; most places do not charge, but in those that do, the charge generally per person (about 40p to 90p), so it is wise to ask ahead as this can clearly add up for a large party. It is always a good idea to telephone in advance to check opening times of restaurants, as they vary considerably.

$$$	Expensive (above £30)
$$	Moderate (£20–£30)
$	Inexpensive (below £20)

Bloomsbury

North Sea Fish Restaurant $ *7 Leigh St., WC1; Tel. 0207/387 5892.* Upmarket fish and chips restaurant offers sardines, salmon and sole as well as classic British fish and chips. All major credit cards.

Townhouse Brasserie $$ *24 Coptic St., WC1; Tel. 0207/636 2731.* Modern European menu features a wide variety of inventive nouvelle dishes, with excellent French desserts. Good wine list, too. All major credit cards.

Chelsea

Bluebird **$$$** *350 King's Rd., SW3; Tel. 0207/559 1000.*
Fashionable Terence Conran restaurant with a café and upscale
food store attached. Modern British menu with Pacific Rim
influences. Expensive and noisy; reservations necessary. All
major credit cards.

Como Lario **$** *22 Holbein Place, SW1; Tel. 0207/730 9046.*
Old-style Italian food, good atmosphere with loyal regulars.
Situated just off Sloane Square. All major credit cards.

The English Garden **$$$** *10 Lincoln St., SW3; Tel. 0207/584
7272.* Newly renovated neighborhood favorite in an unusually
beautiful setting, serving the latest in modern as well as traditional British cuisine. All major credit cards.

Gordon Ramsey **$$$** *68–69 Royal Hospital Rd., SW3; Tel.
0207/352-4441.* The celebrity chef's eponymous establishment
has earned two Michelin stars and continues to gratify gour-
mands with an ever-changing *prix-fixe* menu. Reserve one
month in advance, even for lunch, as the place is very small. All
major credit cards.

Vingt-Quatre **$** *325 Fulham Rd., SW10; Tel. 0207/376 7224.*
As its name implies, this popular restaurant serves good hot
meals all day and night. Excellent choice for after the pub clos-
es, or when up all night with jet-lag. All major credit cards.

The City

Sweetings **$** *39 Queen Victoria St., EC4; Tel. 0207/248 3062.*
Traditional 150-year-old fish restaurant. Small and immensely
popular with the City lunch crowd, so prepare to wait in line.
Lunch only, no reservations accepted. Cash only.

London

Chinatown

Chuen Cheng Ku $$ *17 Wardour St., W1; Tel. 0207/437 1398.*
This large, busy restaurant is one of the best places in London to try *dim sum* (served until 5:45pm). All major credit cards.

Fung Shing $$ *15 Lisle St., WC2; Tel. 0207/437 1539.* High-quality food is served in this authentic Cantonese restaurant. All major credit cards.

Mr. Kong $$ *21 Lisle St., WC2; Tel. 0207/437 7341.* One of Chinatown's leading restaurants, serving innovative dishes as well as old favorites. All major credit cards.

Wong Kei $ *41 Wardour St., W1; Tel. 0207/437 6833.* Enormously popular Chinese restaurant. Always noisy and hectic; expect to share a table. Cash only.

Covent Garden

The Calabash $ *38 King's St., WC2; Tel. 0207/836 1976.* Located in the basement of the Africa Centre, serving African cuisine. All major credit cards.

Food for Thought $ *31 Neal St., WC2; Tel. 0207/836 0239.* A tiny basement restaurant serving vegetarian dishes. Changing menu every day, but the vegetables with brown rice are a good standard and excellently priced. Cash only.

The Ivy $$$ *1 West St., WC2; Tel. 0207/836 4751.* Although it can take months to get a reservation at this celebrity hangout, the exquisite Modern European food makes it worth the wait. All major credit cards.

Rules $$$ *35 Maiden Lane, WC2; Tel. 0207/836 5314.* London's oldest restaurant serving traditional English fare. A historical landmark whose one-time patrons include Dickens, Thackeray, and Edward VII. All major credit cards.

Simpson's-in-the-Strand $$$ *100 Strand, WC2; Tel. 0207/836 9112.* Superlative traditional food in Edwardian surroundings. *The* place in London for roast beef and Yorkshire pudding. Tip the meat carver. Jacket and tie required. All major credit cards.

East End

Arkansas $ *Spitalsfield Market, E1; Tel. 0207/377 6999.* For Americans homesick for genuine barbecue, this is the place to go. The prize-winning American chef makes the best ribs in Europe. MasterCard and Visa only.

Golders Green

Bloom's $ *130 Golder's Green Road, NW 11; Tel. 0208/455 1338.* London's most acclaimed kosher restaurant. All major credit cards.

Solly's $$ *148A Golders Green Road, NW11; Tel. 455 0004.* The 1st-floor restaurant here is supposedly Europe's largest kosher restaurant; downstairs is less exotic with a counter and takeaway service. Good Middle Eastern cuisine. All major credit cards.

Kensington

Launceston Place $–$$ *1A Launceston Place, W8; Tel. 0207/937 6912.* Charming, country-house atmosphere serving impeccable modern European cuisine. All major credit cards.

Phoenicia $–$$ *11 Abingdon Rd., W8; Tel. 0207/937 0120.* Excellent Lebanese and Middle Eastern food. Go at lunch time for the all-you-can-eat buffet. All major credit cards.

London

Wodka $–$$ *12 St Alban's Grove, W8, Tel. 0207/937 6513.* Polish restaurant offering well-made classics, as well as good European and vegetarian dishes. Nice atmosphere, and an amazing vodka menu. All major credit cards.

Knightsbridge

Fifth Floor $$$ *Harvey Nichols, 109 Knightsbridge, SW1; Tel. 0207/235 5250.* Fine contemporary cuisine served at the top of London's most fashionable department store, *prix-fixe* lunches; serves dinner too. All major credit cards.

Sale e Pepe $$$ *9 Pavillion Rd., SW1; Tel. 0207/235 0098.* Good solid Italian food served in an amusing atmosphere of controlled chaos, that includes the surprising "special" cappuccino. All major credit cards.

Veg $ *8 Egerton Garden Mews, SW3; Tel. 0207/584 7007.* Very good prices at this Szechuan vegetarian restaurant that makes meat-free classic Chinese dishes such as the excellent Peking "duck." Great for dinner, but order off the menu during the lunch buffet. Cash only.

Vong $–$$ *Berkeley Hotel, Wilton Place, SW1; Tel. 0207/235 1010.* Southeast Asian menu featuring fresh ingredients and imaginative cooking at this fine restaurant in one of Knightbridge's upscale hotels. All major credit cards.

Zafferano $$$ *15 Lowndes St., SW1; Tel. 0207/235 5800.* Home to possibly the best tiramisu in London, Zafferano has a dedicated following among foodies in the know, due to the inventiveness of the menu and the artful simplicity of the cooking. All major credit cards.

Marylebone & Regent's Park

Woodlands $ *77 Marylebone Lane, W1; Tel. 0207/486 3862.* Excellent Southern Indian vegetarian cuisine. All major credit cards.

Mayfair & Piccadilly

Connaught Restaurant $$$ *Carlos Place, W1; Tel. 0207/499 7070.* Housed in the grand Connaught Hotel, this restaurant provides a rare glimpse into a more gracious time, when service was king and the customer was treated as one. Superb French and English food. All major credit cards.

Le Caprice $$$ *Arlington St., SW1; Tel. 0207/629 2239.* Fashionable, if plainer, sister restaurant of the Ivy, with equally great food and celebrated customers. All major credit cards.

Chez Nico at 90 Park Lane $$$ *90 Park Lane, W1; Tel. 0207/409 1290.* Here is an elegant dining room in which to enjoy a menu of exquisitely high-quality classic French food, with a smart-casual dress code. All major credit cards.

Le Gavroche $$$ *43 Upper Brook St., W1; Tel. 0207/408 0881.* This comfortable basement restaurant is the setting for truly world-class French *haute cuisine* served impeccably. Best deal is the set lunch. Jacket and tie. All major credit cards.

Gaucho Grill $$ *19 Swallow St., W1; Tel. 0207/734 4040.* Devoted to Argentinian beef, the Gaucho Grill serves some of the best steaks in town in a South American atmosphere. Vegetarian dishes are available. All major credit cards.

Mirabelle $$$ *56 Curzon St., W1; Tel. 0207/499 4636.* Chef Marco Pierre White's most successful restaurant serving magnificent classic French mixed with traditional British food. Features a garden and affordable prices, both quite unusual for this area. All major credit cards.

Momo $–$$ *25 Heddon St., W1; Tel. 0207/434 4040.* Moroccan *tagines,* couscous, and other flavorful foods served in an Arabian Nights decor, by beautiful young waiters to a night-time crowd of beautiful young customers. Good lunch-time deals. All major credit cards.

Veeraswamy $$ *99–101 Regent St., W1; Tel. 0207/734 1401.* The oldest and most upmarket of London's Indian restaurants, opened in 1927, and has been nicely updated. All major credit cards.

North London

Lemonia $ *89 Regent's Park Rd., NW1; Tel. 0207/586 7454.* Popular Greek-Cypriot restaurant with a lively atmosphere and excellent food. Reservations are essential. Does not take Amex or Diners Club.

Mango Room $ *10 Kentish Town Rd., NW1; Tel. 0207/482 5065.* Great local place for Caribbean food near London's very hip Camden Market. Good music, atmosphere, service and prices. Booking advised. Does not take Amex or Diners Club.

Odette's $$ *130 Regent's Park Rd., NW1; Tel. 0207/586 5486.* Modern European cuisine in one of the most charming and romantic townhouse restaurants around, with Odette's Wine Bar in the basement and a conservatory upstairs. Menu changes daily. All major credit cards.

Notting Hill & Portobello

Clarke's $$–$$$ *124 Kensington Church St., W8; Tel. 0207/221 9225.* Highly acclaimed modern cuisine by *artiste* chef Sally Clarke. *Prix-fixe* menu only on weekday evenings. All major credit cards.

First Floor $$ *186 Portobello Rd., W11; Tel. 0207/243 0072.* Modern, international cuisine in a trendy establishment on Portobello Road. Menu changes daily. All major credit cards.

Geales $ *2–4 Farmer St., W8; Tel. 0207/727 7969.* Cheap and cheerful fish restaurant. Terrifically popular, and for good reason. All major credit cards.

Julie's $$ *135 Portland Rd., W11; Tel. 0207/229 8331.* Creative, modern European cuisine in a chic restaurant with a lovely covered courtyard. All major credit cards.

Soho

Gay Hussar $–$$ *2 Greek St., W1; Tel. 0207/437 0973.* Fine old-fashioned establishment serving hearty Hungarian fare. A haunt of politicians and literary folk. All major credit cards.

Lindsay House $–$$ *21 Romilly St., W1; Tel. 0207/439 0450.* Superb Modern British cooking in a charming 17th-century establishment. Outstanding value *prix-fixe* lunch; extensive wine list. All major credit cards.

Mezzo $$$ *100 Wardour St., W1; Tel. 0207/314 4000.* The set-lunch at £15 may be the best way to enjoy this otherwise over-priced Terence Conran restaurant. Modern European with various oriental-inspired dishes. All major credit cards.

Mildred's $ *58 Greek St., W1; Tel. 0207/494 1634.* Small, busy vegetarian joint with good falafel and veggie burgers. Good value. Cash only.

Saigon $$ *15 Frith St., W1; Tel. 0207/437 7109.* Do-it-yourself table-top barbecue at this sophisticated Vietnamese restaurant serving the trendy Soho set. All major credit cards.

London

Sugar Club **$$** *21 Warwick St., W1; Tel. 0207/437 7776.* Antipodean chef Peter Gordon has brought some unheard-of delights to the table here, including kangaroo. Masterful cooking with an unusual menu of food that justifies the high price. All major credit cards.

South Kensington

Bibendum **$$$** *81 Fulham Rd., SW3; Tel. 0207/581 5817.* Set in the beautiful Art Nouveau Michelin building, Bibendum's reputation stretches far and wide. Restaurant upstairs, oyster bar downstairs. Book for dinner at least two weeks in advance. All major credit cards.

Bombay Brasserie **$$** *Courtfield Rd., SW7; Tel. 0207/370 4040.* One of London's best and most atmospheric Indian restaurants. The eat-all-you-like lunch buffet is very good value. All major credit cards.

Cambio de Tercio **$$** *163 Old Brompton Rd., SW5; Tel. 0207/244 8970.* Excellent food at this stylish Spanish restaurant with huge *tapas* selection, and unusually good desserts. All major credit cards.

Itsu **$–$$$** 118 Draycott Ave., *SW3; Tel. 0207/584 5522.* Spend a little or spend a lot here, depending on how hungry you are. A conveyor belt carries little plates of sushi, sashimi, vegetables, hot dishes, and desserts around two circular bars at this sleek and popular restaurant. All major credit cards.

Poisonnerie de l'Avenue *82 Sloane Ave., SW3; Tel. 0207/589 2457.* An elegant restaurant whose top-grade fish and excellent chef keep the wealthy locals coming back again and again. All major credit cards.

INDEX